Philomel Books
An imprint of Penguin Random House LLC, New York

First published in the United States of America by Philomel Books,
an imprint of Penguin Random House LLC, 2022

Philomel Books is a registered trademark of
Penguin Random House LLC.

Visit us online at penguinrandomhouse.com.

Library of Congress Cataloging-in-Publication Data is available.

Manufactured in Italy

ISBN 9780593621028

10 9 8 7 6 5 4 3 2 1

LEGO

Edited by Jill Santopolo
Design by Rory Jeffers

Text set in Mercury.
Art was created with gouache, ink, colored pencil, and crayon.

The CRAYONS TRICK or TREAT

PHILOMEL

DREW DAYWALT   OLIVER JEFFERS

The Crayons are ready
for Halloween.

They can't wait to fill
their bags with treats.

You know what you're supposed to say on Halloween, Right?

OF COURSE WE DO.

Orange knocks
on the first door.

Green knocks on
the next door.

Oh, it's HALLOWEEN!
And WE have to be polite too.

Oh, <u>POLITE!</u>
okay WE get it now

Gray knocks on
the door after that.

It's a <u>SCARY</u> holiday Everyone!

OH SCARY! OK I got this one!

White knocks
on the door.

That's not quite
what I meant...

It WAS close, though.

Gray steps
forward again.

WAIT!

Repeat after me:
Trick. Or. Treat.

There we go.

The crayons all
knock on the door.

And also... *BOO!*

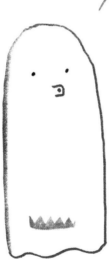